White Wave

A CHINESE TALE

Retold by DIANE WOLKSTEIN

Illustrated by ED YOUNG

Gulliver Books

Harcourt Brace & Company

San Diego   New York   London

To Jinx Roosevelt, woman of light,
for her gift of friendship —D.W.

To JoAnn King for her spirit, light, and guidance,
and Kwok Ming for his friendship —E.Y.

Library of Congress Cataloging-in-Publication Data
Wolkstein, Diane.
White wave: a Chinese tale/retold by Diane Wolkstein;
illustrated by Ed Young.
p.   cm.
Summary: Kuo Ming's discovery of a moon goddess inside
a snail shell changes his lonely life.
ISBN 0-15-200293-6
[1. Folklore—China.] I. Young, Ed, ill. II. Title.
PZ8.1.W84Wh   1996
398.2'0951'01—dc20   95-451

Printed in Singapore

A B C D E

The illustrations in this book were done in graphite pencil on paper.
The display type was hand rendered by John Stevens.
The text type was set in Weiss.
Color separations were made by Bright Arts, Ltd., Singapore.
Printed and bound by Tien Wah Press, Singapore
Production supervision by Warren Wallerstein and Pascha Gerlinger
Designed by Judythe Sieck

AUTHOR'S NOTE

As I was coming out of the British Museum in London in 1976, I was caught in a sudden summer thunderstorm. I ducked into the Atlantis Bookshop for shelter, and a bright yellow book titled *The Goddesses of India, Tibet, China, and Japan* by Lawrence Durdin-Robertson (Cesara Publications, Enniscorthy, Ireland) beckoned to me from the back bookshelf. As the thunder rolled in the distance, I leafed through the book and was caught again—this time by the Chinese story of White Wave.

The instant I read "White Wave," I thought of Ed Young. In 1975 he had asked me to write the text for the Persian story *The Red Lion*. I loved Ed's art and wanted to reciprocate by offering him a story he might want to illustrate. Not only was Ed intrigued by the challenge of rendering a celestial being visible, but he remembered the story from his childhood in Shanghai. Before beginning his sketches for the book, Ed came to hear me tell "White Wave." We spoke again about his memory of the story. I spoke with other Chinese people who knew the story, and it evolved with each new telling. In 1979 our book *White Wave* was published.

This revised edition of *White Wave* is a wonderful example of the intermingling of past and present, of the oral tradition and the printed word. The changes in this edition are a result of the responses of the hundreds of audiences who have listened to the story since 1977, as well as the subtle editing of Liz Van Doren and Alison Hagge. When my editors at Harcourt Brace suggested that I give the farmer a name, I asked Ed if he had a preference. Ed then told me that when he did the original sketches for the book, he was drawing his longtime friend Kuo Ming. When I asked him what Kuo Ming meant, he replied, "Country Bright." "Perfect!" I said, delighted with the continual living mystery of the story. Stories transform and change us, and we in turn change and transform them. Just as the name of the heavenly being in the story was at first unknown and then revealed, so, too, the unknown farmer has now been given a name.

"White Wave" belongs to a group of Asian stories sharing the motif of the celestial being who descends for a short time to earth, chooses a mortal to bless, and then returns to heaven.

Kuo Ming is pronounced Kwo Ming.

—*Diane Wolkstein*

In the hills of southern China, there once stood a shrine. It was made of stones—beautiful white, pink, and gray stones—and was built as a house for a goddess.

Now the stones lie scattered on the hillside. If you should happen to find one, remember this story . . . of the stones, the shrine, and the goddess White Wave.

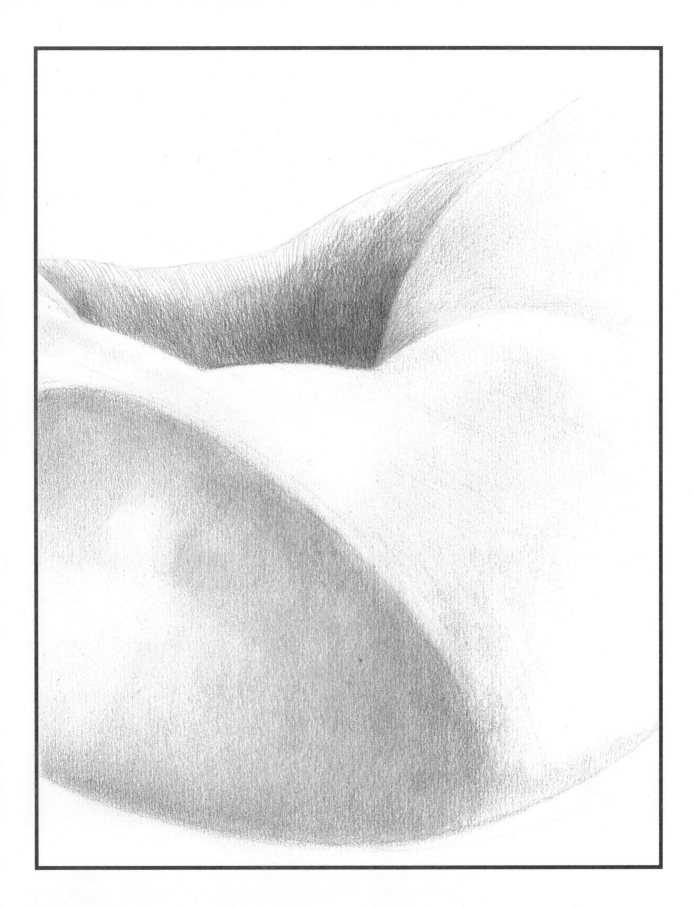

LONG AGO, in the time of mysteries,
a young farmer was walking home from
the fields in the evening. He walked
slowly, for he was not eager to return to
his house. He lived alone. His parents
had died two years before. He was too
poor to marry and too shy to speak with
any of the young women in his village.

As he passed through a small forest,
he saw a stone, a beautiful white stone,
gleaming in the moonlight.

The young man, whose name was Kuo Ming, bent over to look at the stone. It wasn't white. It was every color in the rainbow. And when he held it in his hands, he saw it wasn't a stone at all but a snail, a moon snail. And what was the most wonderful good fortune—it was alive!

The farmer gently carried the snail home and placed it in an earthenware jar. Then, before fixing his own dinner, he went out again and gathered fresh leaves for the snail.

The first thing he did the next morning was to look in the jar. The leaves were gone. The snail had eaten them. Kuo Ming picked four more leaves and went off to the fields to work.

When he came home that evening, the farmer found his dinner waiting for him on the table—a bowl of cooked rice, steamed vegetables, and a cup of hot tea.

He looked around the room. No one was there. He went to the door and looked out into the night. No one. He left the door open, hoping that whoever had prepared his dinner might join him.

The next evening his dinner was again waiting for him—and this time there was a branch of wild peach set in a vase on the table. The farmer made a special trip to the village to ask if strangers had arrived. No one knew of any.

Every morning he left leaves for the snail. Every evening his dinner was waiting, and always there was a wildflower in the vase.

One morning Kuo Ming woke up earlier than usual. He took his rake and started off as if he were going to the fields. Instead he circled back to his house and stood outside the window, listening. There was no sound. Then, as the first light of the day touched the earth, he heard a noise.

He looked in the window and saw a tiny white hand rising from the jar. It rose higher and higher. Then a second white hand rose from the jar, and out leaped a beautiful girl.

She was pure light. Her dress was made of silk, and as she moved her dress rippled, changing from silver to white to gold. Wherever she stepped in the room, the room shone.

He knew, though no one had told him, that she was a moon goddess. And he knew, though no one had told him, that he must never try to touch her.

The next morning, before he went to work, he watched her, and the next morning, and the next.

As the days went by, his loneliness
disappeared. He skipped to the fields
in the morning and walked quickly
home in the evening. His dinner was
always waiting. The house was shining.
The air was sweet. And his heart was
full.

Many days passed. Then, one morning,
as he was watching her sweep the floor,
her long black hair fell across her face and
a great longing came upon him. He wanted
to touch her hair. The desire burst upon
him so strongly and quickly that he forgot
what he knew. He opened the door and
rushed into the room.

"Do not move," she said.

"Who are you?" he asked.

"I am White Wave, the moon goddess. But now I must leave you, for you have forgotten what you knew."

"No!" he cried.

"Good farmer," she said, "if you can hold yourself still and count for me, I will leave you a gift. Let me hear you count. Count to five."

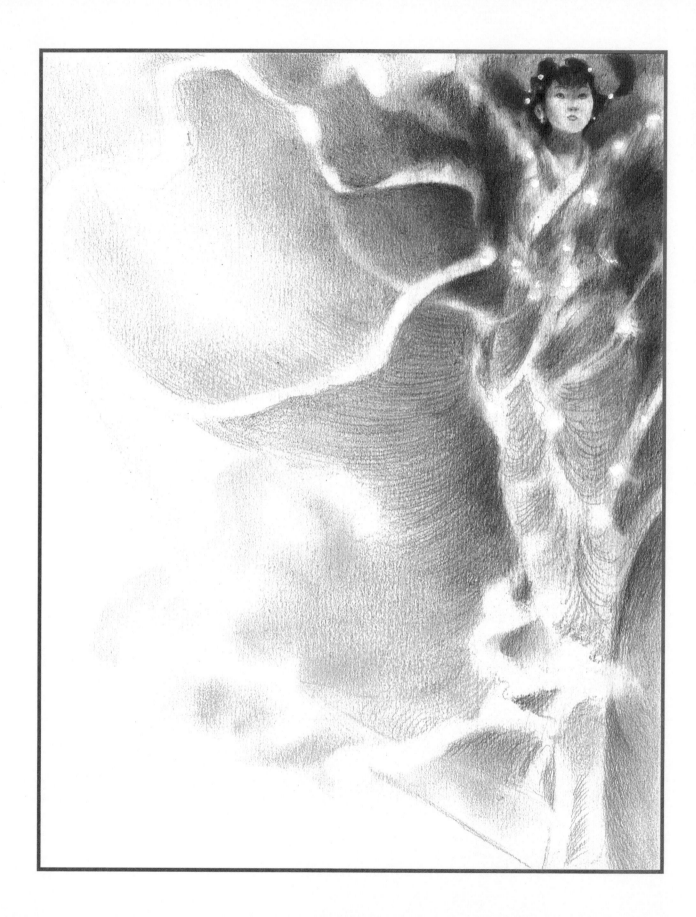

"One," he whispered.

She crossed in front of him and walked toward the open door.

"Two," he said softly.

"I leave you my shell."

"Three," he said more strongly.

"If ever you are in great need, call me by my name, White Wave, and I will come to you."

"Four," he cried.

There was a streak of lightning and a great roll of thunder.

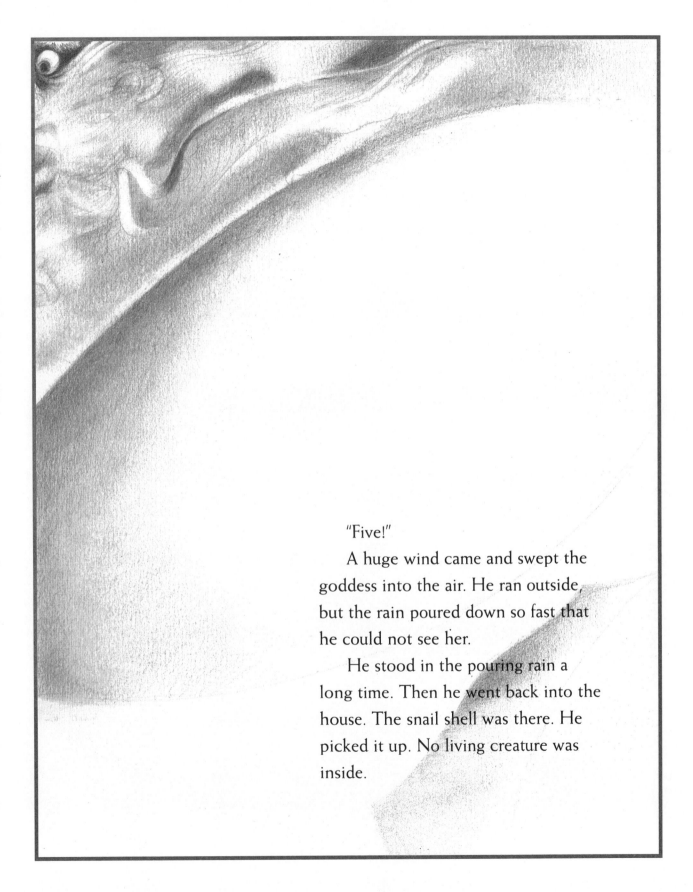

"Five!"

A huge wind came and swept the goddess into the air. He ran outside, but the rain poured down so fast that he could not see her.

He stood in the pouring rain a long time. Then he went back into the house. The snail shell was there. He picked it up. No living creature was inside.

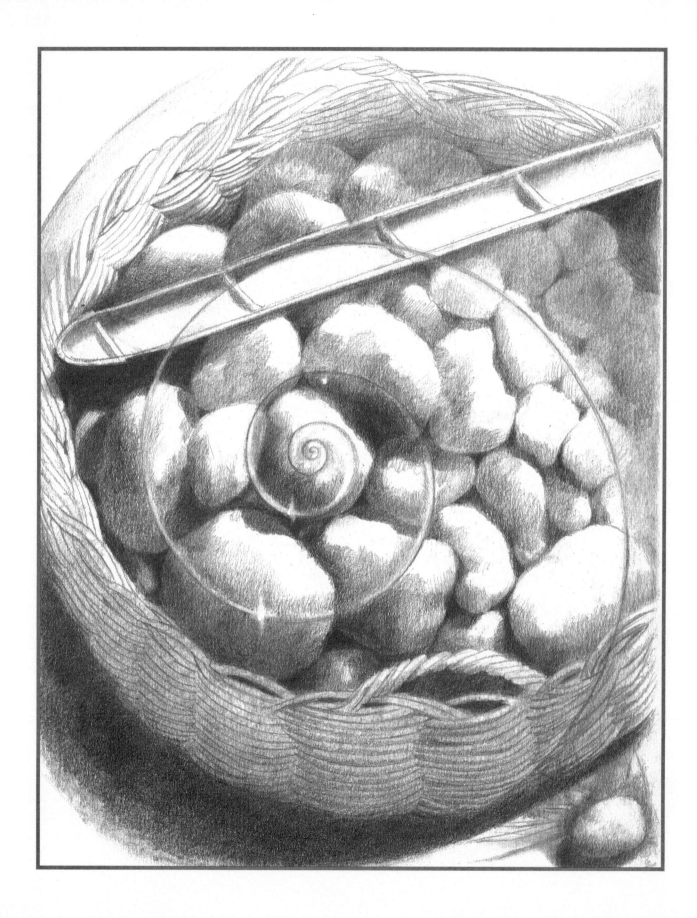

Kuo Ming went to the fields, but he did not think of his work. He thought only of White Wave and how to bring her back.

As he was wandering over the hills, his foot struck a stone. He bent over to look at it. At that moment, he decided he would build a shrine for White Wave—a beautiful stone house where she might live peacefully. He spent more time choosing the stones—beautiful white, pink, and gray stones—than working in the fields. When the harvest came, it was very small. He ate the little there was. He ate the supplies he had stored, and after that he lived on berries and wild grass.

At last, one evening, the shrine was complete. But that evening the farmer was so weak with hunger, he could barely walk. He stumbled into his house and tripped over the earthenware jar. The shell fell out.

Quickly he picked it up, and as he held it, he remembered the words of the goddess: "If ever you are in great need, call me by my name, White Wave . . ."

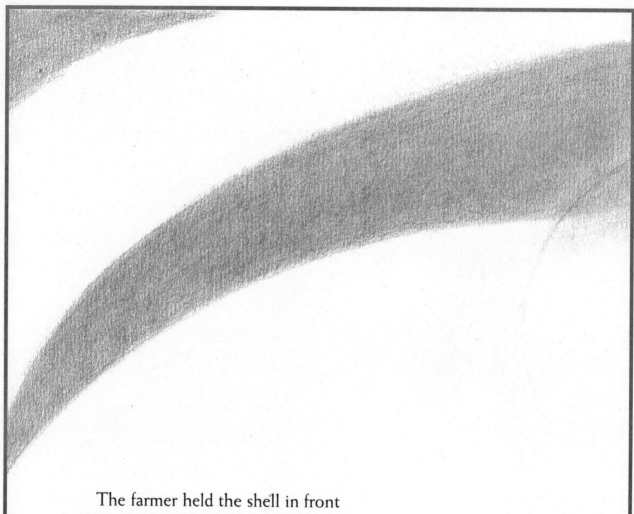

The farmer held the shell in front
of him. Then he raised it in the air, and
with his last strength he cried: *"White
Wave, I need you."*

Slowly he turned the shell toward
him. A wave of gleaming white rice
cascaded out of the shell and onto the
floor. He dipped his hands into it. The
rice was solid and firm. It was enough
to last him until the next harvest.

He never called her name again. With the flowing of the rice, a new strength had come to him. Kuo Ming worked hard in the fields. The rice grew. The vegetables flourished. He married and had children. But he did not forget White Wave.

He told his wife about her, and when his children were old enough, he took them on his knee and told them the story of White Wave. The children liked to hold the shell in their hands as they listened to the story.

The shrine stood on the hill above their house. The children often went there in the early morning and evening, hoping to see White Wave. They never did.

When the old man died, the shell was
lost. In time the shrine, too, disappeared.
All that remained was the story.

But that is how it is with all of us:
when we die, all that remains is the story.

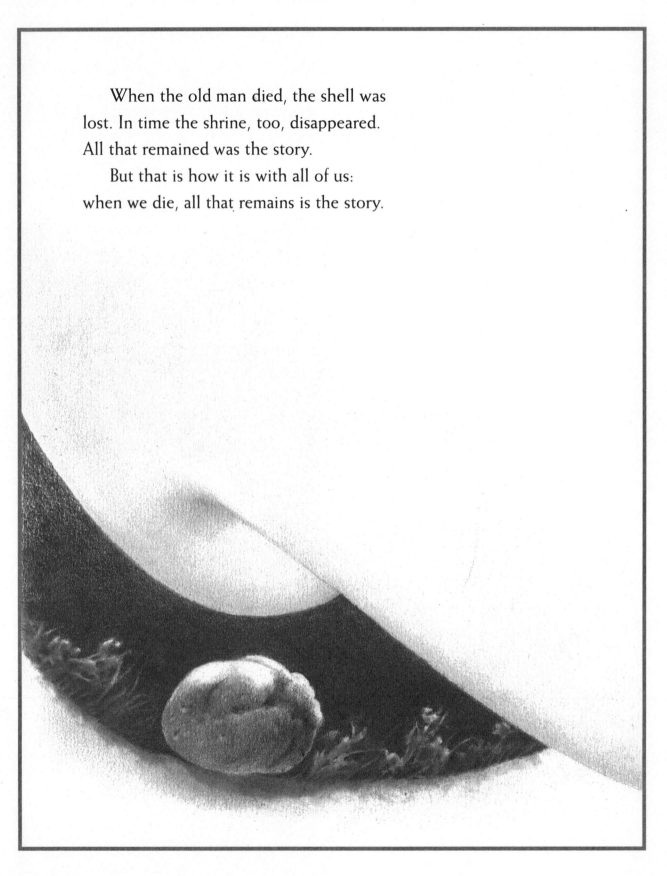